Dear Parent:
Your child's love of reading starts here!

Every child learns to read in a different way and at his or her own speed. Some go back and forth between reading levels and read favorite books again and again. Others read through each level in order. You can help your young reader improve and become more confident by encouraging his or her own interests and abilities. From books your child reads with you to the first books he or she reads alone, there are I Can Read Books for every stage of reading:

SHARED READING
Basic language, word repetition, and whimsical illustrations, ideal for sharing with your emergent reader

BEGINNING READING
Short sentences, familiar words, and simple concepts for children eager to read on their own

READING WITH HELP
Engaging stories, longer sentences, and language play for developing readers

READING ALONE
Complex plots, challenging vocabulary, and high-interest topics for the independent reader

ADVANCED READING
Short paragraphs, chapters, and exciting themes for the perfect bridge to chapter books

I Can Read Books have introduced children to the joy of reading since 1957. Featuring award-winning authors and illustrators and a fabulous cast of beloved characters, I Can Read Books set the standard for beginning readers.

A lifetime of discovery begins with the magical words "I Can Read!"

Visit www.icanread.com for information
on enriching your child's reading experience.

To the Messler kids—Jude, Ollie, and Kendall—
from their neighbor and fan
—J.O'C.

For Ben
—R.P.G.

To D.D.—une canard femelle extraordinaire
—T.E.

HarperCollins®, ✿®, and I Can Read Book® are trademarks of HarperCollins Publishers Inc.

www.icanread.com
Library of Congress Cataloging-in-Publication Data is available.
ISBN 978-0-06-123610-5 (trade bdg.) — ISBN 978-0-06-123609-9 (pbk.)
14 SCP 20 19 18 17 16 15 14 13 12 ❖ First Edition

I Can Read!™

BEGINNING
1
READING

Fancy NANCY
and the Boy from Paris

by Jane O'Connor

cover illustration by Robin Preiss Glasser

interior illustrations by Ted Enik

HarperCollins*Publishers*

I almost always get to school early.

But on Monday I am tardy.

(That's a fancy word for late.)

I come in and see a new kid.

He is standing next to Ms. Glass.

"Robert comes from Paris!"

Ms. Glass is telling everyone.

"He just moved here."

Paris!

Paris is a city in France.

It is gorgeous.

(That is a fancy word for beautiful.)

"*Bonjour,*" I say in the book nook.

(In French that means "hello.")

"I am Nancy.

I never met anybody

from Paris before."

I speak slowly so he will understand.

"It's really nice there," Robert says.

"I miss it."

He has a book on cowboys.

He probably wants to learn

all about this country.

"I want to go there someday."

I show him my book.

It is about a dog in Paris.

"Do you like the United States?"

"Yes," says Robert. "Don't you?"

"Yes, I do," I say.

"I've lived here all my life."

Then Ms. Glass puts a finger
to her mouth.

"This is not talking time," she says.

"This is reading time."

On Tuesday

I sit next to Robert at lunch.

"Have you ever been

to the Eiffel Tower?"

I ask him.

12

Robert nods and swallows.

"Lots of times.

Our house was near it."

I tell Robert,

"I know about the Eiffel Tower.

There's a poster of it in my room.

I know lots about Paris."

I share some of my lunch.

"These are donut holes," I say.

Robert gives me a funny look.

"I know that.

I have eaten donut holes before."

That night

I tell my mom and dad about Robert.

"He is very nice.

He already speaks English.

I want to be his friend.

How do you say friend in French?"

"The word is *ami*," my mom says.

"You say it like this: ah-mee."

I love French.

Everything sounds so fancy!

"Why don't you ask him

over to play?" my dad says.

So the next day I do.

"We can play soccer.

Did you play soccer in Paris?"

"Sure. All the time," Robert says.

"I am a good kicker.

I can come on Friday."

On Thursday it is Show and Share.

Robert brings in a toy horse.

It is brown and white.

"My grandpa has a horse like this."

Then Robert passes around a photo.

"I miss her a lot.

Her name is Belle.

In French that means beautiful."

"Belle," I say to myself.

Now I know another French word.

On Friday Mom is at work.

Mrs. DeVine picks us up from school.

"Mrs. DeVine lives next door,"
I tell Robert.

"Robert is from Paris,"
I tell Mrs. DeVine.

At home

we make a tent in the yard.

We pretend bears are outside.

We pretend to be terrified.

(That's a fancy word for scared.)

Then we play soccer.

We let my little sister play too.

Robert is a great kicker.

My dog runs around the yard.

"That's Frenchy," I tell Robert.

"She is not really French.

But you will like her anyway."

We go inside and

I show Robert my room.

"See? There's the Eiffel Tower,"

I say.

"Yes," says Robert.

"But that one does not
have a cowboy hat on it.
That Eiffel Tower is in Paris, France.
It is taller, and it is more famous.
But we have an Eiffel Tower too.
Our Eiffel Tower has a cowboy hat
on the top."

Wait a minute! I am very perplexed.
(That's a fancy word for mixed up.)
"But you're from Paris, France," I say.
"Aren't you?"

"No, I am from Texas.
Paris, Texas," Robert says.
"Ms. Glass told everybody
that the first day."
Robert shows me Paris, Texas,
on my globe.

Oh!

I guess I missed that part.

And I feel a little silly.

But not for long.

After all,

I have a new *ami*,

even if he isn't French.

Fancy Nancy's Fancy Words

These are the fancy words in this book:

Ami—"friend" in French (you say it like this: ah-mee)

Belle—"beautiful" in French (you say it like this: bell)

Bonjour—"hello" in French (you say it like this: bohn-joor)

Gorgeous—beautiful

Perplexed—mixed up

Tardy—late

Terrified—scared